# Pucker
## and the Difficult Day

Illustrations by Nigel Chilvers

**EGMONT**

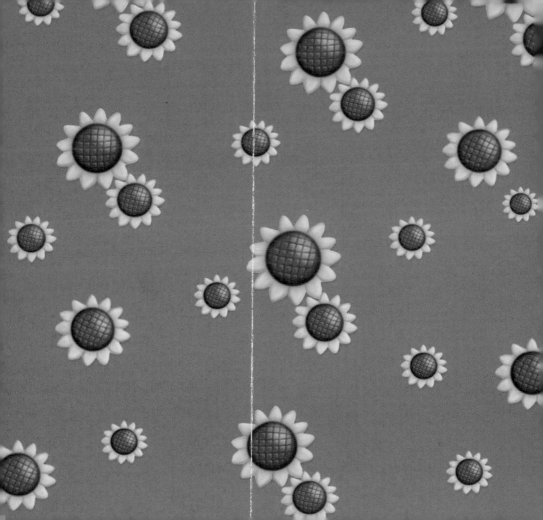

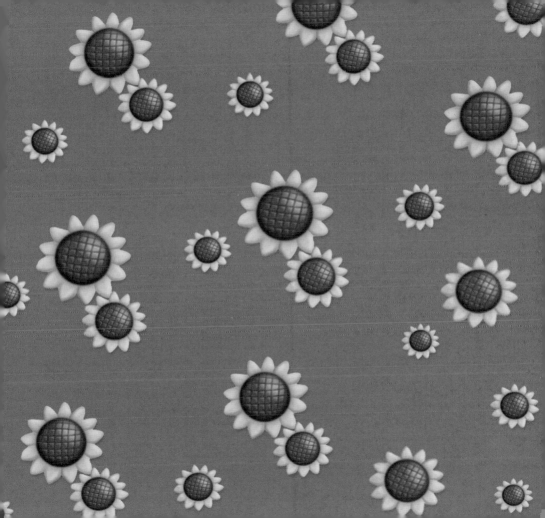

# EGMONT

*We bring stories to life*

First published in Great Britain 2009
This edition published in 2010
by Egmont UK Limited,
239 Kensington High Street, London W8 6SA
Endpapers and introductory illustrations by Craig Cameron.

HiT entertainment

ISBN 978 1 4052 4341 4

1 3 5 7 9 10 8 6 4 2

Printed in Malaysia

A new face has arrived in Sunflower Valley – Farmer Pickles' delivery truck, Packer. His first day is very busy! Will he cope with all the deliveries?

Things were getting very busy at the Sunflower Valley depot.

"I'm worried about all these deliveries," said Travis. "It's a lot to do, what with my farm work and all." But Travis didn't have to worry for long. With a loud blast of a horn, a cheery red truck arrived.

"Are you Farmer Pickles?" he panted, out of breath with excitement. "I'm Packer – your new delivery truck!"

Packer could not wait to start work. "Pack me up and watch me go, go!" he sang eagerly.

Farmer Pickles showed Packer his two special trailers. "First you have to collect the seaweed from the seaweed farm," Farmer Pickles said, "then deliver it to Mr Sabatini's restaurant in Bobsville."

But Packer was so keen to get going that he forgot something important . . .

At the farm, Annie Pickles was loading seaweed into crates when Packer zoomed up and bellowed a loud, "Hello!"

"Erm, Packer," said Annie, slowly, "where's your trailer?"

Oh dear! In all the excitement, Packer had forgotten to bring it with him.

"Don't worry," Packer mumbled, "I'll . . . I'll go and get it now. Sorry."

And off he raced.

Packer sped through Sunflower Valley, worrying what Farmer Pickles would say about his mistake.

"I'll just have to work extra hard," Packer decided as he skidded into the depot.

Packer hooked up his trailer. "Collect and deliver! Collect and deliver!" he chanted, zooming off again. But he stopped when he saw Mr Sabatini's bakery.

"Wow! A bakery!" he smiled.

"You must be-a Packer," said Mr Sabatini. "My bread is ready for delivering!"

"Delivering, that's my job!" beamed Packer. "Pack me up and watch me go, go!"

"It all-a needs to go to my restaurant in Bobsville," said Mr Sabatini. "Thank you."

"That's where I'm taking Annie's seaweed," Packer remembered. "Ooh! I've still got to collect the seaweed!"

With the bread safely loaded into his trailer, Packer set off for the seaweed farm. But which road led to the sea? Packer couldn't remember!

He met Spud by the roadside, shooing away some crows. The honking of Packer's horn soon scared them away! "Which way's the sea?" asked Packer.

"Don't worry, Spuddie will show you!" Spud beamed eagerly.

Back at the seaweed farm, the seaweed still hadn't been picked up. Annie called Farmer Pickles on the talkie-talkie. "Packer went to get his trailer," she told him, "and he hasn't come back yet!"

So Farmer Pickles rang Mr Sabatini, who was not happy! "That-a Packer! He-a take-a my bread but he-a hasn't delivered it to Bobsville! Where has it gone?"

Poor Farmer Pickles didn't know!

Just then, Bob called Farmer Pickles. He wanted Travis to collect some supplies from the docks.

"I'll get my new truck, Packer, to go," said Farmer Pickles.

"Thanks, that's brilliant!" said Bob happily.

"I just need to *find* Packer first," Farmer Pickles sighed to himself.

A long time passed. Finally, Packer arrived at Scarecrow Cottage. Farmer Pickles was waiting for him. "Where have you been?"

"I'm sorry," spluttered Packer. "I forgot my trailer, so I had to go back. Then I saw the bakery, and then I lost the road . . ."

"And found me!" Spud chipped in.

Farmer Pickles chuckled. "I know you're excited, but you must concentrate!"

Packer worked extra-specially hard after that. He raced back to the seaweed farm and collected the seaweed from Annie.

Next, he zoomed to Mr Sabatini's restaurant to deliver the seaweed *and* the bread.

Then Packer hurried back to the depot to load his flatbed trailer with crates of sunflower oil, to be taken to the docks.

"I'm collecting and delivering!" he sang.

Packer was very excited about going to the docks, but the eager truck kept his mind on his work.

The dock workers unloaded the crates of sunflower oil before Packer loaded up his trailer with Bob's supplies. Then he set off back to the yard to deliver them.

"Thanks, Packer," said Bob, "just what we need, and in really good time, too!"

With Bob and Wendy on board, Packer set off for Scarecrow Cottage. Farmer Pickles was waiting with a parcel.

"Is that another delivery?" Packer asked.

But this parcel was for Packer – his very own talkie-talkie!

"You're one of the gang now!" said Bob.

Packer beamed. It was good to have friends who understood how difficult the first day of work could be!

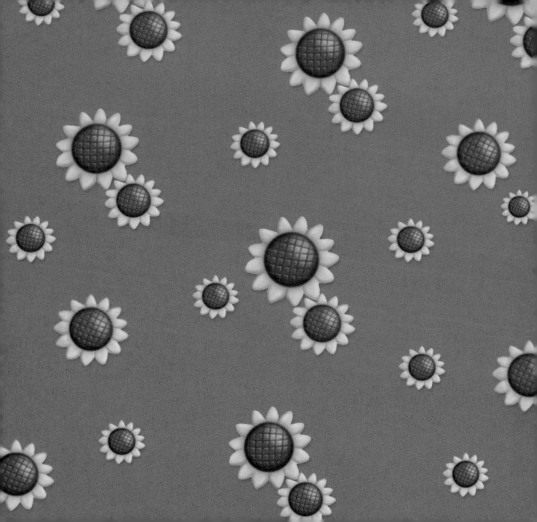

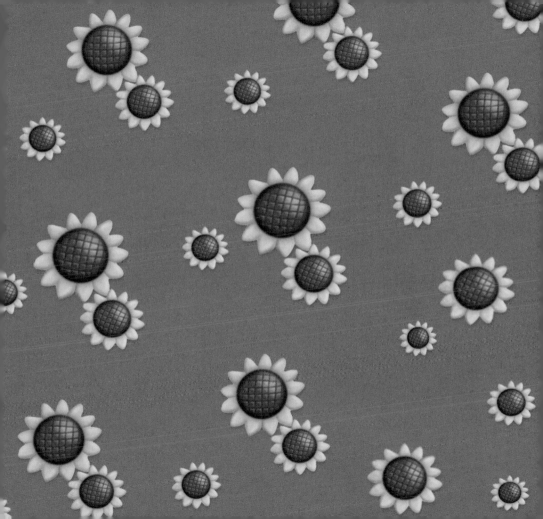